This book belongs to

_____

The
Little Match Girl

BY

Hans Christian Andersen

Retold by Samantha Easton

ILLUSTRATED BY

Erin Augenstine

ARIEL BOOKS

ANDREWS AND McMEEL
KANSAS CITY

Library of Congress Cataloging-in-Publication Data

Andersen, H. C. (Hans Christian), 1805–1875.
    [Lille pige med svovlstikkerne. English]
    The little match girl / Hans Christian Andersen : illustrated by
Erin Augenstine.
       p.   cm.
    Translation of: Lille pige med svovlstikkerne.
    "Ariel books."
    Summary: The wares of the poor little match girl illuminate her
cold world, bringing some beauty to her brief, tragic life.
    ISBN 0–8362–4931–3 : $6.95
    [1. Fairy tales.] I. Augenstine, Erin, Ill. II. Title.
PZ8.A542Lis   1992
[E]—dc20   91–31052
                                             CIP
                                              AC

Design: Susan Hood and Mike Hortens
Art Direction: Armand Eisen, Mike Hortens, and Julie Phillips
Art Production: Lynn Wine
Production: Julie Miller and Lisa Shadid

The
Little Match Girl

It was the last night of the year, and it was a very cold, dark night. The streets were empty. Everyone was home in their warm houses, busily cooking their New Year's Eve feast of roast goose and chestnut stuffing and apple pie and other good things.

Though it was very late, a little girl could be seen still walking slowly down the icy streets.

She had no hat on
her head nor any shoes
on her feet. When she left her house that
morning, she had been wearing a pair of old
slippers that were full of holes. They were far
too big for her, and they had fallen off as she
ran across the street to get out of the way of
an oncoming carriage. One of them had
vanished altogether, and a little boy had run
off with the other one, saying it was so large,
it would make a fine boat for his tin soldiers.

Since then, the little girl had had to go bare-foot, and her little feet were blue with cold.

In her ragged apron, the little girl carried matches, and she held a packet of them in her hand. She was supposed to be selling them, but no one had bought a single match from her all day or given her so much as a copper penny. Now, the child was shivering and faint with hunger as she walked forlornly through the darkness.

Sometimes, she stopped to stare into the lighted windows of the houses along the streets. All the houses were decorated in honor of the New Year. Delicious smells wafted out to the street, making the little girl feel hungrier.

At last, she came to a corner between two tall stone houses that was sheltered from the icy wind.

The little girl sat down there and pulled her feet under her, hoping to warm them. But it did no good. The cold air seemed to sink into her very bones.

The little girl was afraid to go home, for she had not sold any matches that day. She knew her father would probably beat her for that. Besides, it was not much warmer at home than it was outside in the street—the walls of their rooms were so full of holes. Her mother had tried to stuff them with straw and rags, but the wind howled through them as strong as ever.

The little girl stretched out her hands. They were stiff with cold. "If I lit just one of these matches," she thought, "I would feel so much warmer!" She gazed longingly at the packet of matches in her hand. Then she drew one out and struck it against the wall, making a loud scratch. The match sputtered and flared, casting a bright, clear light.

The little girl stared at it. All of a sudden, it seemed to her that she was sitting in front of a big iron stove with feet of brightly polished brass. Inside, a coal fire blazed brightly.

How warm and beautiful that fire was! Eagerly, the little girl stretched out her hands toward it. She pulled out her little bare feet to warm them by the glowing embers of the wonderful fire. But just then, the match went out.

The big iron stove vanished, and the little girl found herself on the cold, dark street again, holding a half-burned match in her hand.

The little girl pulled out another match and struck it. The flame rose, casting a light on the stone wall beside her. Suddenly the walls looked as transparent as glass.

It seemed to the child that she could see right through the wall into a room. There was a long table covered with a snow-white cloth and set with fine china, crystal glasses, and silver forks and knives and spoons. In the center, an enormous platter held a steaming roast goose stuffed with apples and sausage. How delicious it looked!

Then, something even more wonderful happened. The goose leaped off the platter, and with a knife and fork still stuck in its breast, came walking toward the little girl. She reached out her hands toward it. But as she did so the match went out.

Once again everything turned dark, and the little girl found herself staring only at the damp stone wall.

As quickly as she could, she pulled out another match and struck it.

This time the light blazed forth even more brightly, and the little girl found herself gazing up at an enormous Christmas tree.

It was much larger and more splendidly decorated than any Christmas tree she had ever seen. Even the ones she had glimpsed through the windows of rich people's houses could not compare with it.

Hundreds upon hundreds of lit candles gleamed in its green branches. Colored pictures of angels hung from it—pictures such as those the little girl had sometimes seen in shop windows at Christmastime. Only these pictures were even more lifelike and far more beautiful.

The child stretched out her hand toward the tree. Just then the match flickered out. But as the little girl watched, the candles on the Christmas tree seemed to rise higher and higher, until she realized she was staring at the stars in the sky.

They twinkled down at her so brightly and looked so beautiful she felt as if her heart would break. Then she saw one of them fall, leaving a bright trail of light behind it.

"Somebody must be dying," the little girl thought. Her grandmother, the one person in the world who had ever truly loved her, had once told her that whenever a star falls it means a soul is rising to heaven.

The little girl pulled out another match and struck it against the wall. This time, the light flared up in front of her, forming a bright circle like a halo.

In the center of it stood the little girl's grandmother. She looked so radiant and loving that the little girl could not help but cry out to her.

"Oh, Grandmother," she said. "Please take me with you. I know that when the match goes out you will vanish, just like the big warm stove and the lovely roast goose and the beautiful Christmas tree. Oh, Grandmother, please don't leave me here. Don't, please!"

And as the match burned out, the little girl desperately clutched the packet and struck the rest of the matches against the hard stone wall. They burst into flame, and

together they made a light that seemed brighter than the noonday sun.

In the blazing light, the little girl saw her grandmother again. The little girl stretched out her hands, and her grandmother gently took the child in her arms.

Then together they rose high above the dark icy streets to a place where there was no more hunger, no more cold, and no more pain or suffering. They rose all the way to heaven.

Early the next morning some passersby came upon the little match girl.

She was still sitting in the corner between the two houses, leaning against the wall. She was smiling but her small cheeks were pale, for she had frozen to death during the night. "Oh, the poor child," the people mourned.

Some of the people pointed at the bundle of burnt matches the child held in her hand. "Look!" they said. "The little creature must have tried to warm herself!"

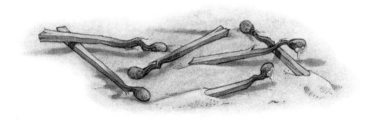

But they could not possibly know all the wonders the little match girl had seen that night. Nor would anyone know how joyfully she and her grandmother had celebrated the coming of the New Year.